bees, snails, & peacock tails

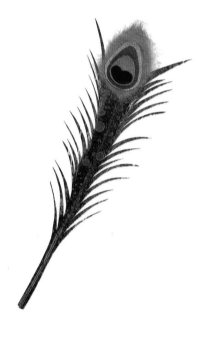

bees, snails, & peacock tails

Patterns & Shapes . . . Naturally

Betsy Franco

Illustrated by Steve Jenkins

Margaret K. McElderry Books

New York London Toronto Sydney

Margaret K. McElderry Books

An imprint of Simon & Schuster Children's Publishing Division

1230 Avenue of the Americas, New York, New York 10020

Text copyright © 2008 by Betsy Franco

Illustrations copyright © 2008 by Steve Jenkins

Book design by Sonia Chaghatzbanian

The text for this book is set in Lomba.

The illustrations for this book are collage.

Manufactured in China

10 9 8 7 6 5 4 3 2 1

Library of Congress Cataloging-in-Publication Data

Franco, Betsy.

Bees, snails, & peacock tails: patterns & shapes . . . naturally / Betsy Franco ; Illustrated by Steve Jenkins.—1st ed.

p. cm.

ISBN-13: 978-1-4169-0386-4

ISBN-10: 1-4169-0386-0

1. Nature—Poetry. I. Jenkins, Steve, 1952– ill. II. Title.

PS3556.R3325B44 2008

811'.54—dc22

2006012094

FIRST
EDITION

*For Hari and Michael, my
wonderful sister and brother.*

*Thank you to Michael Elsohn Ross,
a fellow writer and naturalist,
who kindly advised me on this book.*
—B. F.

For Jamie
—S. J.

In the day
    and the night,
    on the land
and in flight,

    tucked in hollows
        of trees,
        in the tide pools
    and seas,

    you'll find patterns and shapes—
    from the snakes to the bees!

Study a beehive
and you will see
the mathematical genius of the bee.

The hexagons

you'll find inside

fit side

by side

by side

by side.

This math
is passed

mysteriously

from worker bee

to worker bee!

Moths show their symmetry
every spring,
flitting at night
on fragile wings.

Notice the colors
and stunning "eyes,"
perfectly matched
on either side.

Attracted to windows
or candlelight,
moths are kaleidoscope shapes
in flight.

Some spiders weave
delicate tapestries
that shine in the sunlight
and sway in the breeze.

They spin lacy lines,
then go round
and round.

Their knowledge of shapes
is truly profound.

They sit in the center
admiring their art,
and wait for those flies
who aren't quite as smart.

If you should meet a peacock pair,

the male's the one with all the flair.

The female, who is rather plain,

is dazzled by his patterned train.

She watches as he struts and preens,

his fan a blaze of blues and greens.

Look up in the sky and seasonally
you'll notice it's filled with graceful Vs.

A knowledge of angles
helps migrating birds
to fly with less effort
and also be heard.
By forming a wedge,
the swans and the geese
slice through the air
and travel in peace.

When a foraging ant leaves a scent on the ground,
then the worker ants know where the food can be found.

In a very straight line they march home with the snack,
knowing, piece by small piece, they can carry it back.

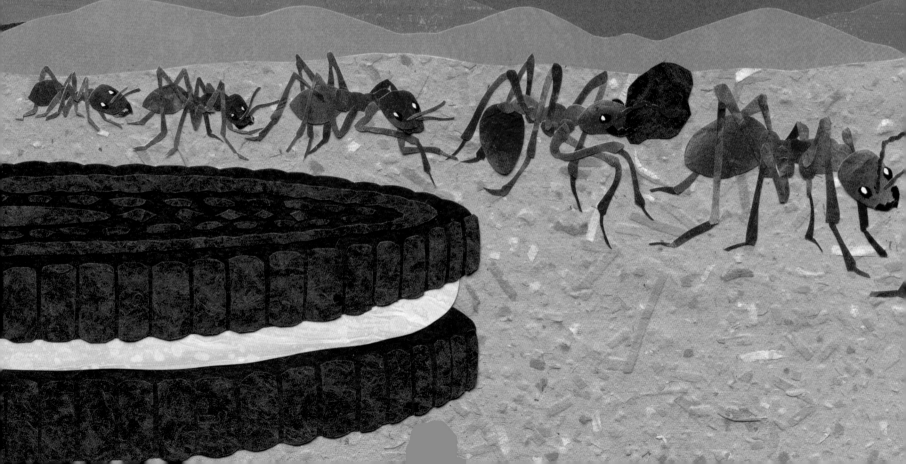

In careful formation they travel along—
their deep sense of teamwork is inborn and strong.

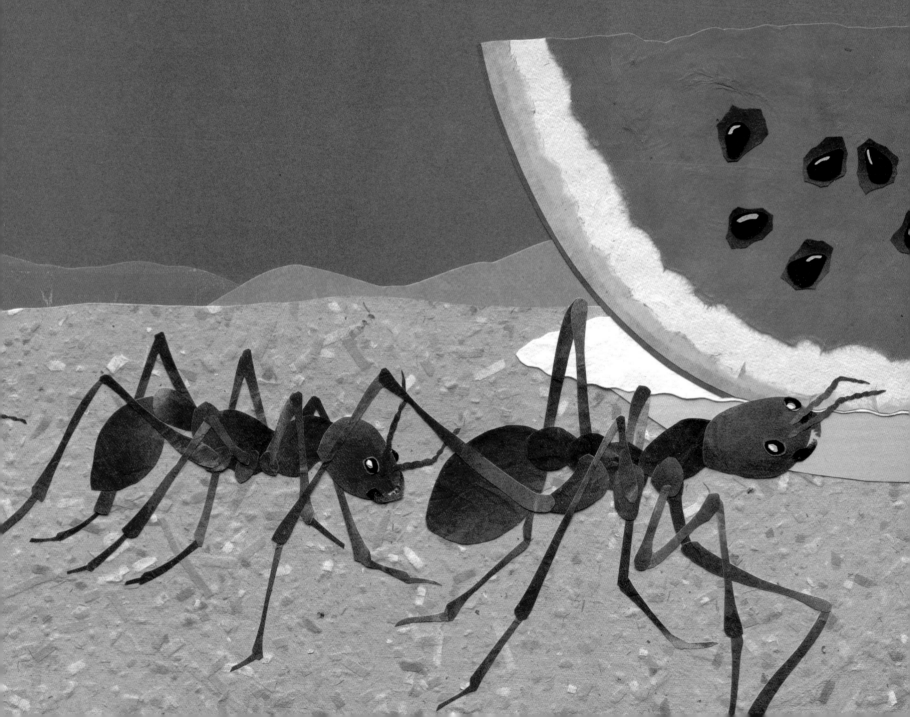

By moonlight, a mouse
        who is bounding around
leaves delicate prints
        all over the ground

in a pattern of four
        that repeats and repeats—
two tiny front paws,
        two bigger back feet.

On the dirt or on snow
        the pattern you see
makes the mouse part of
        nature's geometry,

as he scurries about
nibbling acorns and seeds,
and occasional insects—
whatever he needs,

till an owl takes flight
to dine for the night.
Then the mouse and his footprints
head out of sight!

On diamondback snakes
and on copperhead snakes
you'll recognize diamond and triangle shapes.

The snake rubs its nose on a branch or a rock,
then takes off its skin like a knee-high sock.

Off comes the old skin and waiting below,
repeating designs appear in a row.

Sea stars have five arms,
 or six arms, or more,
with sensors called "eyespots"
 that help them explore.
They grow back an arm
 if they get into scrapes,
for they take such great pride
 in their bright, starry shapes.

The animal known as the puffer fish does **not** want to be someone's gourmet dish. Whenever it senses there's something to fear, it puffs itself up till it's almost a sphere.

The beautiful spirals on topshell snails are miniature castles with tiny details. The spirals go round, getting wider and wider till you get to the snail—the shell's insider!

So there you have it. . . .
I think you'll agree

that creatures
  on land,
  in the air,
  in the sea

make patterns and shapes
quite naturally!

New Angles
on the
Animals

bees

In one day, worker bees can build thousands of wax cells in their honeycomb. Each cell has a hexagon shape, which makes it strong and gives the honeybees lots of space to store nectar and pollen.

moths

Moths that have eyespots usually rest with their wings flat, rather than closed. This makes it easy to see that the designs on the wings are symmetrical. The "eyes" are thought to frighten away predators.

spiders

Orb-weaver spiders first spin a framework and straight lines. Then they finish off the web with a sticky spiral of thread that creates amazing geometric shapes. The center of the web, where they sit, is dry.

peacocks

The male peacock's tail feathers are called a *fan* or a *train*. Dotted with eyespots, his fan is one of the most spectacular in the world. He struts around and displays it to attract a mate.

migrating birds

When birds fly in a V formation, the flapping of a bird's wings gives a lift to the bird behind it. They take turns being the leader because leading takes the most energy.

ants

Living in colonies, ants know how to work together and share. When forager ants find food, they bump their abdomens on the ground, leaving a scent trail for other ants to follow.

mice

The tiny deer mouse is only 2 1/2 to 4 inches long. When it bounds around, its back feet land in front of its front feet. This shows up in its footprints. Sometimes a deer mouse even leaves a tail print.

snakes

The shapes and patterns on the diamondback and copperhead snakes are made of scales. Baby snakes grow rapidly, making it necessary for them to shed their skin as many as seven times a year.

sea stars

Sea stars with five arms are the most common, but some have more. One example is the sunflower star, which can have more than twenty arms. At the tips of their arms, sea stars have sensors that detect light.

puffer fish

When a puffer fish feels threatened, it gulps water and puffs up to about twice its size. Although it moves more slowly in this form, it is much harder to swallow.

sea snails

Sea snails known as ringed top shells carry their homes on their backs. They have one foot, like a suction cup, which helps them grip onto and move along seaweed, rocks, and other surfaces in the ocean.